T A R I F A

TARIFA

a short novel by

JEAN COQT

translated from the french by

charles lunaire

the second part of

Skagen a novel of Europe

for Eve

ISBN: 978-0-9907588-1-5

Healdsburg : Ear Press : 2014

Contents

1. Car. Carryl. Carpenters.

FEBRUARY. BEHIND THE BEACH where the coast road curves a bit to accommodate a low but intrusive hill, that's where the old fort rots away, by day and by night, no one at all concerned. A dusty railroad track. Shaggy palms. An abandoned bicycle lying on its side in the weeds like a dead donkey. Further on the road is full of water, full of water, from one side to the other and well beyond, the pavement hidden beneath a shining reflection of the luminous grey sky overhead. Overhead, having no choice.

The road is full of water and the car goes slower, much slower. In theory this is not very safe: anything might be hidden beneath the water on the pavement: rubbish, a dead animal, something fallen off the back of a truck, a fallen bicycle. Or there could be nails: buildings are under construction, carpenters' trucks pulled up in the soft ground at building sites. Still there's a careless kind of pleasure driving through these long stretches of flooded roads, and the pavement has been first-rate since reaching the coast, no potholes, and the location of the invisible pavement easy to guess, equidistant between shoulders clearly indicated by posts, shrubs, the palm trees evenly spaced on each side, like feather dusters balanced on the ends of their ornately turned dark brown handles, as Carryl points out...

The American girl quiet in the back seat: what does she think. Does she think in Spanish or English. Probably both; probably Spanish if thinking of a Spanish subject, English when contemplating those in the front seat, the driver intent on slowly parting the floodwaters, Moses at the

Red Sea, the woman at his right, looking out her window at the rhythmically passing evenly spaced palms.

La ciudad la mas vieja, she is thinking, having heard him announce that it is the oldest settlement in Europe, the first colony established by the Phoenicians as they beat their way around the Mediterranean, traders and alphabeteurs, hugging the coastline as all sailors then did, no reason to tempt the ocean god.   Like any town down here, stucco, dusty even after the rain, white where not stained by tires, or time, or the shoes and trouserseats of unemployed men leaning up against the buildings, backs to the buildings, cigarette, maybe a can of beer in the right hand, squinting with bad eyes, overalls of that startling blue now faded, somewhere a woman to wash them, possibly iron them, having hung them in the sun, further fading them.

He drives quietly, the road now dry again, and thinks of Ulysses washed up on the beach, and the princess playing with her ball, with her attendants.   If you wanted to you could figure out how many generations ago.   Three to a century, let's say; if eight hundred years BC, then three times twentyeight, only eightyfour generations, that's within imaginability.   Three, after all, right here in this car: one twentyeighth the span.   How often had he tried to encourage them to work out sums in their heads: and they don't even know their multiplication tables these days; not one of them knows nine times seven.

Past the old fort, entrance to the city. Park outside.

Stucco buildings on crazy streets, bending for no apparent reason, winding down from the main road into the heart of the town, if the town can be said to have a heart. A bar. A few cars, dented and dirty, not parked so much as simply left here and there. One not even its door closed: Someone drove up, or maybe coasted in, the engine stopped, the door opened — he imagines the sound of metal creaking against metal — a clumsy fellow throws a faded blue leg out, then the other, he pushes against the steering wheel with right hand, left hand on the door, cigarette between his teeth, drags himself into the bar, leaving the door to stand listless and inert, open. And so there are flies in the bar. Flies buzz listlessly over the bar, droning in the background, spotting the glass. The dirty streaked glass over the photo. The men stand at the bar, two of them, cigarettes stuck to their lower lips, another behind the bar, knuckles of both hands resting on the tired plank. The whitewashed plaster wall repeats, unconsciously, the streaked stucco walls outside. Ontogeny recapitulates phylogeny, or is it the other way round. All this seen in silence, like an old movie. And if he were to enter the cafe what would he say anyway; he doesn't speak their language, their languages, and they not likely his. Surely they're locals, they have the look of habitués, not travelers.

He waits, reflecting, for the others to catch up. He is getting nothing done. There has been no writing in the last, oh, ten days at least. No translation in weeks. Everything is on hold, in a holding pattern, as the airplane had been before landing last time in the States, circling the hills north of San Francisco. Perhaps that was Mom's reason for all that traveling, in her last years, to put things on hold, to circle, circle, to delay the landing. Evasion: or at least, delay. It had been a tiring drive, and the walk, down the narrow cobbled street, between white-plastered buildings, toward what must be the center, was relaxing. Time for a beer.

2. Caged birds all around.

HE WANTS A BEER, and he deserves it. I wonder if there will be any tea. Yes, of course, there'll be a wooden box, hinged cover, little compartments, tea bags, Earl Grey, Mint, English Breakfast. Where ever will we sleep tonight. The old woman yesterday crocheting on a chair on her patio, caged birds all around her, the distant hills beyond the city perched high above the ploughed fields. *Pueblos blancos,* Arcos de la Frontera. We might have stayed there, it looked promising, and the *sopa de ajo* which could have used a little more garlic, and the nice braised pigeon. Expensive, but I suppose no more than it was worth, and we might make up for it tonight.

If the bullring could speak, what would it say, in its festive, dusty, oracular voice, its O voice. They have painted me red and white, the first colors, the true primaries. Red white and wood, of that am I made, and open to the sky whose blue goes unremarked, and my floor is sand, white sand. *Arena blanca.* Most hours I am empty, alone, silent; my life like most a length of Nothing punctuated by Somethings. Systole diastole and the pause that refreshes. Alone in the car in the passenger seat between him and the door. Alone on the sidewalk when there is a sidewalk alone in the little streets next to him. Looking at the windows, at the pavement, at the rooftops, at the sky, at him. Alone in the gardens on the footpaths sitting on the benches taking a cup of tea. Alone with my thoughts or without them.

Ruins of a farmhouse, an abandoned farmhouse, destroyed perhaps in the Civil War. He climbed the staircase, once probably inside the building, now completely exposed. No handrail, no walls. He'll fall off if he's not careful. Inside, in the ground floor, a row of bowls carved or molded into a single slab. Concrete, surely, not stone. Outside, the view all around, the dry hills under their supple ridges, contours against a brilliant blue sky. Under them huge expanses of olive groves, perhaps almonds. The town, white town, on its hilltop, with narrow passageways for streets, people sitting out in front of their front doors. Conversation with old woman who'd been crocheting on her patio with caged birds all around. What's that mountain in the distance? Looks like a giant's head, lying on its back, nose in the air.

The electricity missing this morning. Power failure. The boy at the front desk seemed unconcerned; I suppose this my parents and all the time. Breakfast limped along; the kitchen must cook with gas. Suddenly a commotion: two girls have been trapped all this time in an elevator. They'd been knocking and calling but no one heard them until finally it was quiet enough for the guy at the front desk, only a boy, to hear something, and go and investigate. No way to telephone; that's out too. He went upstairs to the first floor, pried open the elevator door, shone a flashlight down at the roof of the elevator cab, somehow got down and opened its hatch and helped them out. They were relieved, untroubled, smiling, ready for breakfast. I suppose this happens all the time.

Something to write home about. Everyone looked smiles at them at breakfast, unable to speak more than a few polite words. They don't speak English; they don't speak Spanish. Where can they possibly be from? They look European. Polish? Ukrainian?

Bandaids which in this country come in one long roll so you can cut whatever width you want — very sensible. Look at

the Egyptian, Greek, & Roman pieces. Moving so quickly
from one to the next, never able to linger, to study one or
another, to give them the attention that anyone would agree
is their due. Not much stays in detail, but from Egypt the
wood sculptures, the baboon group in pink granite, the
mastaba, the astonishingly lifelike scribe, the bull on the
staircase, the Djebel el Arak knife, a number of cats
upstairs. In the Greek galleries the Winged Victory — an
amazing piece, with a marvelous, alive stride, powerful and
animated. The Venus de Milo is not as impressive as the
kneeling Venus of Vienna. Some marvelous male figures,
too: tall, magnificent Apollo, sleeping Hermaphrodite,
beautiful, serene. The greyhound in the south parterre, the
funeral dog in the Egyptian gallery.

He deserves a beer but where will we sleep. Everyone here,
no matter how brokendown he looks, knows where he will
sleep tonight. And who with? They all look like loners
sitting with their glasses, work clothes, but do they work, or
is this siesta time. Of course they may have been talking
before we arrived. Groups of men standing at bars, talking,
joking, falling silent when we arrive, when strangers arrive.
Village behavior. Not hostile, not even suspicious, they
simply live in a different world. A completely different
world. And so they do not drink beer, they don't drink
coffee, they smoke, they drink little glasses of something.

We all looked at the mouse. Wary at first, but purposeful,
he came from somewhere, behind one of the vats I suppose,
haltingly scurried to the tin basin, up the ladder and across
to the sherry was it, funny I don't remember, and how did it
end.

3. A distant dog or two.

VOICES ACROSS THE WATER from men in boats. The slap of ropes against masts, though the water seems hardly to be moving, there is no wind at all, the weather has held remarkably fine for days now, in spite of all the pessimism. It's always like that: You always bring such good weather, they always say. Cycles of predictability, no, predictable cycles of unpredictably sudden events. In the mountains, for example, where it'll be clear for a few days, then begin to cloud over, then the thunderstorm, perhaps violent, then the clearing, repeat first act. Not April Fool's Day a pleasure. Not April at all: typical summer weather.

From the village far below, bells of different pitches, calling and responding; an occasional voice, probably that of a child or a few children; now and then — rarely — a motorbike. The automobiles are generally quieter here. The rooftops: corrugated iron, flagstone, occasionally red tile. The houses scattered about as if by a clumsy but careful giant. Attentive to rules.

A boat in the distance. Bells of different pitches; finches. Little traffic noise — a boat in the distance, its motor barely heard; a distant dog or two, barking at the breeze, at the silence, as if not a human were present. Looking back down on the long sinuous road through its bare landscape, not a car or a person to be seen. The Holy Virgin brought up this long steep hillside, a mountain really, from one distant church to another, a solemn and joyous procession. This is not Spain. The seas are of different colors. Out on the water, somewhere, the sea meets the ocean. To the

west, Cadiz, the long strand, silent isolated men standing or
strolling, one or two with a dog.

Greyhounds: How was the trip?   Well, you know the
Greyhound — stops at every telephone pole and fire
hydrant.   It took days, nearly a week.   Looking out the
window: grainfields, orchards, a river but not very often. A
distant dog or two.   Mountains on the horizon.   On the
mountains, the white cities, and, inland, the curious
mountain resembling the head of a supine giant. I told her

A horse walked methodically among the tables, a tall dark
horse. The rider a handsome sober woman perhaps in her
forties, sober dark clothing, severely dressed hair, unsmiling,
sure of her circuit among the tables under the plane-trees,
methodically dismounting, dropping reins to the ground, no
need to tether this grave horse. She joins a quiet older man
sitting alone with a glass and a bottle of wine. It looks like
a custom. Have I mentioned her hat, a low flat brimmed
one, black like her clothes, like her hair, black grosgrain
ribbon.

Long hunt for our American girl who had gone on ahead
on the gravelly strand, sea on one side, seawall the other, at
irregular intervals, well apart, lone figures, nearly all men,
leaning on the wall, elbows on the stone, chins perhaps in
cupped hands, gazing no doubt out to sea, not seeing,
contemplating something interior, or nothing at all.

Finches and the occasional peremptory sparrow at their
dinner, finding it as they can, when it appears — can they
know how it gets there? Yes, they flock to a newcomer. He
makes the gesture of scattering grain on the pavement;
tricked, they flutter down to the street; disappointed, they
take wing again. Serve him right he gets bombed. Oh,

good luck, they say, when your hair or your hat is soiled; but I don't think so.

The sudden awareness of plants, of vegetation — trees line streets; grasses grow up in neglected pavement. Alarming shrubbery at the edges of rooftops, pointed roofs. In Paris that day, the woman who directed the maintenance of all the public trees in Ile-de-France. Trees line the country roads, she said, because they are beautiful, and because they are useful. Trees in the landscape, even the urban landscape, are like words in a poem. They show the way and they are the way.

The plane-trees, regularly spaced on a grid on the bare sandy patio sloping gently away from the tables. Neatly coppiced by that never-seen gardener, one of those who maintain the cypresses in the Alhambra. Architectural landscape, like dactylic hexameter. The legacy of the Romans everywhere. Discipline, poetry, and arenas.

Glasses of wine. A Fino.

Finches lack concept of work.

Village bells. A few children.

Police, guns on their hips.

4. Another O voice, stone mostly.

A LARGE HEAVY STONE had worked its way through the years to the surface of the street. I know what happens. It's a function of my shape, helped some by my mass. All those vibrations from the traffic: horses, men, carts, trucks, trams, decades of feet. Microscopic vibrations. Sand and gravel settling under one side or the other. They think we neither live nor move: everything present's alive, inexorably moving. Sand and gravel settling under one side or the other, lifting me grain by grain through the detritus to the light. The quantity and quality of detritus. The quality influences, I will not say determines, the rate of my ascent. The degree to which it is compacted, of course; and that has increased over the years, not as much as you might think, the attraction of the earth's center seems more determinate than for example the hooves or wheels, even the tampers. And then the grain. Lifted against another stone I veer one way or another to work around it, a gigantic atom swerving with exaggerated deliberation, if that's not a contradiction in terms. Determinations.

Porto is no different from Tarifa. A little more evolved, perhaps. An abandoned badly ruined house or apartment building, not a very different concept no matter the century. Porto can wait: it is likely to be years, several years. Now Tarifa: the old fort beside the coast highway, and the road leading down to the old city below. Winding a bit of course, and blind curves, the rough plaster walls of building scattered carelessly or impulsively or resentfully thrust up against the street which seems to steal space from the houses, houses whose builders made their community only resignedly, against their wills.   Every shoredweller is defensive: invaders arrive by sea, but overland too, from behind your back. Hence the Norman fort.

This is no place for a festive dinner. There will be no steak and kidney pie. These inhabitants dine meagerly. That place doesn't seem too inviting. Those desires will never be well met. Thus our hotel simply has to do.

The English friend, his dream: buying rope to descend to the dining room, rather than drop many feet into his chair at the table through the hole by the side of his bed. How to find rope in an unfamiliar village, that was his problem. He'd assigned it himself. *Tiene cuerda*, he would say, not troubling to verify it, it sounds right.   That hole was troubling: roughly square, a little smaller than the bedside rug which might have covered it though it would never have concealed it, the rug would have sagged into the hole, it would ultimately have fallen through itself, dropping with a plop onto the chair, casual upholstery. And the edges were not smooth, they had been roughly sawn. Vision of Gully Jimson: not the vision I had. And this end of the rope, what to secure it, what to tie it to, to hold back his weight as he slid fireman-style down to the dining room.

A healthy birth is what is proposed, a quick and safe delivery, with attendants to clean everything up, maintain a pleasant environment. The tables under their thin, aged linen cloths, baronial plate indicating the settings, chargers retired for the moment.   Candles; chandeliers; lamps; sconces. *Luxe, calme, et volupté.* Massive heavy clumsy serious wooden chairs, stolid oak, faded striped satin upholstered seats. Menus the size of, well, let's say a small newspaper sheet, in thick board covers, maroon, thin leather. Few choices as expected, and many of them no doubt not available tonight, tonight in quotes. *Man muss ess'.* We will eat. *Comemos amigos.*

In one corner an old Victrola, concealed within it a CD player. Now and then the waiter, stiff, old, apparently tired, no, simply reserving his stamina, pauses by the Victrola, hand tentatively poised, eyes lifted in order first to scan the dining room next to gaze out the one window not curtained over finally to stare blankly into the distance perhaps thinking of Afric not that far away, Afric's dusty strand. The music is stuck; even sprinkling salt on the CD doesn't help. I go upstairs to get my laptop to show them photos to prove our authenticity, well, to support our claim: see: we too are peasants, *somos campesinos tambien.* The laptop gives the game away.

Rain begins to fall a little before eight. So we'll sleep. We'll be up at seven o'clock.

5. Cypress trees all around.

LEADING A MARCH up the street, past the walls, along the hedge, the village idiot, tall and rangy like those shabby cypresses, disheveled really — can you disbelieve it? — banging a wooden spoon against the bottom of a pot, and behind him a raggedy line of children, mostly boys but a few girls too, short pants, skinned knees, elbows flailing, flashing eyes, disciplined disorder. In Barcelona children had been roped together; in Zamora they simply held onto a rope; here they are *uit de lijn*, off leash. What unspoken, unknown social instinct maintains the line, the mostly even spacing of these children. What archaic buried memory permits the adults to stand benignant by, indulging their children and this fool.

As if a steep mountain trail to the summit, this street up the hill to the park. Do you like this garden, which is yours? See to it your children don't harm it! General life; wallpaper patterns. Quietly now, respectful, they descend the steps between the balustrades, water coursing down the troughs of the handrails, ceramic cording — what else to call it? — tucked under the troughs. What cunning; what impeccable work and imagination. You'd swear the fool could see it, appreciate it. Beyond his grasp, but not his reach. Perhaps one of these dusty children, one day, two even, may grow to comprehend.

A rope to belay the litter! shouted the Phoenician! Windy sea, biting wind; a coracle bobbing, bouncing on the blue, nothing wine-dark here. She comes ashore, her dainty slipper reaches for the sands. I hope to betray the leader, flouting the finishers arriving next, floor-scrapers and dishwashers, their oracle nodding, drowsing, uninterested in such prosaic events. Unopened betrayal letter, out and completed, run ashore, faint thrips and mealy-worms among the roses on the beaches and the strands. No hope to restrain the reader, muttered the technician, his alphabet throbbing. Her fainting sister's hands. No.

A railway causeway beyond the leather, the leather seats exposed in the open phaeton. What kind of car is it might be called a Phaeton? Come away, lest your faint simper reach the open doors between their curtained side-rooms. A caged bird, no, a parrot, once irascible, becalmed. The host stands, smiling, welcoming. They walk across the sandy parking court, it all seems like slow-motion, a movie made so long ago, before sound, before color. Twenty rooms, no more, and one for them. A pleasant dining room, a bar, a parrot, the phaeton, her slipper.

A schoolroom in Granada, containing hostile demonstrators, detained *en masse* among the litter. Newspapers every day (not Sunday) discuss such things, these are troubled times. Shout out, you Phoenician! Moroccans, Berbers, Canarians, from across the windy sea, biting the hands that give them succor. *¡Ay corazón te quiero!* A thin violin sounds in the street, plaintive in the plaster corner, that architectural armpit between bar and bodega: *ahí, corazón, quierooo...* You see, I say, they sigh... She can't be more than nineteen years old, certainly no virgin, not yet ready for children, for duty, for keeps, no.

This could be the place to consider loss, real loss. Whole pages missing. Those finishers, they arrive with culture and destruction, alphabeteurs and incendiaries. Even a nineteen-year-old can teach: for keeps, no, out of reach. You'll see, later: the standing stones retooled, herms to helmets.   Everywhere you look, stones in rows, bollards, menhirs, henges, alignments.   Far to the north, beyond the Visigoth chapel, the cave at Altamira tells a different story. The obsessive irrelevance of the Vallée des Merveilles.   Yet today the stroke of a finger eradicates paragraphs.   Her dainty slipper reaches for the beach.

Men push their low flat cart slowly across the packed earth, thin tall discs of wheels creaking on the axles.   From one tall cypress tree to the next.   On the cart, the high ladder, a Giacometti sculpture, or Miró, or Martin Puryear, it doesn't matter who, none of those will show up for another thousand years and then some.   This is the real thing, a tall wooden ladder on a low wooden cart within thin high wooden wheels, men pushing from behind, towing from in front.   Cypress trees all around, like the stones at Carnac. Beautiful, yes, and useful: they show the way.   The trees at Het Loo: look: they remind the citizens of the harmony of difference.

Things are different here, where cypresses and orange groves and olive trees are constant reminders of the Roman grid, the alignment of repeated elements all of the same genera.   In the orange grove the gardener moves slowly, slowly, the grove cool in the hot day.   Deep blue sky, dark green leaves overhead, black green trunks of orange trees standing at regular intervals in the grey beige sand underfoot.   He calmly, methodically directs the water flowing gently through the channels, removing or replacing tiles gating this watercourse or that.   He knows where the water comes from, but it's not his concern.   Presumably his decisions are similar to those of the engineers of the aqueduct, only the scale is different.

Or you could say that the grids, the aqueducts, the corners, the T-junctions with their tile gates letting the water course this way and that, the running words in their graceful lines (arabesques!), the cypress trees all around, the expression of harmony in ratio, these are all network, man and nature mind architecture.

6. Flicks his napkin.

SAN FRANCISCO IS FAR from here.   In any case, the saints
are not so important here in the south.   Teresa, Santiago,
Ignatius, all those northern Christians, descendants of
Visigoths.   Al Andaluz preserves the cosmopolitan Roman
tolerance: pay your taxes, don't question government,
otherwise think, believe, teach whatever you like.   Room for
Mithras, even, and the mother goddess.   Let's say we've lost,
oh, twelve hundred years.   At court, in the marketplace, you
have Jews, Muslims, Christians, freethinkers, all puzzling
over the same eternal question, how to live with pleasure
without causing pain.   Some work at desks, drawing quills
or brushes across parchment, styli through beeswax: others
in the gardens, maintaining the lines and the *acequias*.   A tile
here, a tile there.   Square thin precise measured tiles.

An onion for lunch and wine for conversation, and there at
the main streetcorner stood the fool with his little *gaita*, the.
Fool from Galicia, Visigoth no doubt, ranting about Jesus
between sweet outbursts of bagpipes.   The only way to
silence him: strike up a conversation.   Well, others have
taken their turns, now I'll take mine, first for luck a bite of
this nice crisp onion.   *¿Bo día, parvo, como está hoxe?* No? Not
Galician?   No fooling?   He stands there, bagpipe at ease,
grinning.   Hair every which way, monkeyface, crooked
teeth.   Good morning, Fool, how are you this morning?
¿Nesta fermosa maña? And a fine morning it is and has been,
not yet too hot, water playing in the fountain and a fine
crisp onion.
Japanese prints would not portray a flatter streetscene nor
one in colors more subtly drawn, which reminds me when

and if I disengage from this fool, won't someone else come along, there's a new blue to try out, so I've heard, in the next *diseño*...

Importance risks losing Presence if it overlooks Detail, just as big countries risk provincialism by regarding smaller nations as inconsequential. Just so, each of us gains by attending to the tiny events which, whether at random or to purpose, inform the meaning of our days. Lucretius did his best to understand the forces of Nature, finding more satisfaction in scientific observation and logical inference than ever he found in old stories of the gods. If some of his conclusions seem quaint today, *De rerum natura* remains

No one else in the street, and the fool is not really listening. *On the Nature of Things* remains both true and useful — useful above all — because it is art. Still he is not listening, and threatens to resume the *gaita*. Should have been a wineskin. Artists and poets, I say, artists and poets and fools supply the cement that binds inferences and events, otherwise too small to be seen, into presences attuned to human ear and eye, bearing messages from an invisible source, invisible source.

Javanese prince could rot beneath the adder were it not for those three ladies, a fatter, still fleet thing. Schikaneder and his simpleminded show, so popular with the man in the street. Is this what this fool really wants. Why not just ask him?

Most art elevates the matter beyond the crowd — which remains, transfixed by its own credulity. This fool and his feathers, *gaita* dangling at his side, onion scent in the air. Well: no point in standing here in the middle of the street though it is empty, sun directly overhead, table and chairs under the trees, garçon leaning in the doorway, park the bagpipes and sit, let's discuss this like gentlemen, surely one of us retains sufficient credulance. Garçon lifts an eyebrow, flicks his napkin at a housefly, black and small on the whitewashed plaster doorway.   Thirty cents will buy a decent meal and I've already had my onion bread and wine is all we need. A bit of ordinary sausage, cheese too if you please.

Tintin and the Secret of Literature cannot be far from here. The little man, exchanging places with a fool.   Fools carrying things: valises, baskets, satchels, birds'-nests, containers of every kind.

A sheet of metal, the front panel removed from a washing machine, leaning up against the trunk of a plane-tree, and behind it an unseen insect rasping away as if it mattered. One day it will surely be noticed, carried away.

That was the day of the Tucson shootings. Impossible, you say? Suspend disbelief ye who enter, sit with me under the tree a glass for you a glass for me.

Still: Lucretius knew. Think it over, won't you?

7.   A baker's dozen.

SEVEN REAL OYSTERS, Claires, flown I suppose from Paris. I think they raise them near Carnac, where we traveled once. From which we had a delicious dinner, paté & vin de Provence, duck sautéed *au naturel*, turnips and carrots, coffee afterward. Absurd to sit in Madrid recalling Aix. If I had a nickel for each time this happens...

Right down the street, at the corner, a discreet plaque on the wall: Miró lived here. A short benign man with an affable air, round face, sober suit, clean-shaven, slicked hair. You just never do know what innocuous little man will dream up a revolution. An englishman, only a boy, with his violin, somewhere between Valencia and Tarifa.

He made his way with his fiddle, on foot, from Galicia to the Costa del Sol. Those were the days, my friend, when a ready smile, an obliging tune, youthful honesty and a good deal of endurance would do you through thick and thin, living on not your wits but your optimism. They call him a holy fool.

No time here to lean against a doorway: runners, aptly named, rush up and down two flights of stairs. Is here no dumb-waiter? Meanwhile the real waiters, full of suave patience, pose, poised, at the table-sides, secure in their position, in total control. Diners deal with ancient oversize menus, unsure of their ability to choose.

Voice, oddly loud voice, from another table: whereupon I went back to Beaubourg to make the preceding appointment. Oh, really, she inquires, lifting an eyebrow, preceding? He sets down knife and fork, levels a gaze. Should I have said previous, the previous appointment. But it had already been made, you know. There is no way to make this clear.

Back in the apartment, looking at sketches (Matisse, Laurencin, Marquet, Picabia, Picasso) while the duck *restes* simmered, recalling the dinner at Botin. That idyllic time in Paris, a previous appointment; this idle time in Madrid. The American girl in Salamanca, perhaps at the university, studying the fine ceiling, starbursts of inlaid wood, mudejar woodwork if that can be.

It's mostly downhill from here, at least today, she thinks, lunch behind her, the streets are still quiet, no one's abroad. Siesta time. Even the birds, the starlings and sparrows, have paused for the afternoon. That time in Girona, cannon going off in the evening as we looked for our hotel. Does this go on all night? Oh no, Señora, it will soon stop, it's only to scare away the birds...

This dubious regularity irritates more than it allays. Carefully planned schemes can easily go awry. Unforeseen errors abound: misspellings, mispronunciations, false cognates. Pleasant surprises delight the unsuspecting *bon vivant*. Excited lovers meet in favorite neighborhood bistros. Every good boy does fine — and girls? Counting your words won't save you now. Qualified things act on their direct objects.

The birds, the birds bring all these things together, angels mediating earth and sky. Even the absence of birds can do this work. There are things no one, not the fool with his *gaita*, can accomplish alone, or with any other human, or dog or donkey. It's only the birds, their inscrutable purpose, their unfathomable flight, their uncountable numbers.

Flicks his napkin at a housefly, turns and enters the restaurant, emerges after a minute with two decks of cards. *Tiene señor.* Fool and limner, interrupted in their silent conversation, lift their eyes. The garçon offers the two decks of cards. They're soon removed from their sleeves, the scribe offers them to the fool, the fool taps them benignly.

The limner-scribe cuts the deck clumsily, there are too many cards for his delicate hands, shuffles them awkwardly, offers the deck again to the fool who gravely touches them once more. The garçon coughs discreetly into his white napkin, tosses it back over his left shoulder, bows slightly, turns, and returns to the doorway, leaning absently against the doorframe.

She pauses under the plane-tree, squeezing her handbag between her upper arm and her side, thinking of Lauren Bacall, wanting a cigarette, watching the two men at their cards. A boy played the violin softly, a tune he'd heard in Galicia. Four o'clock in the afternoon. She'll be alone for three more hours at least. Every detail in the scene she contemplates seems to have fallen into place, an architecture of the mind. There are no dogs in the streets. The men have fallen silent, looking at their cards. The boy plays on.

8. Buying rope.

ROUNDING A BEND in the street we came upon two men and a metal wheelbarrow.   The men were in work clothes; the wheelbarrow was nude, unpainted, undecorated, dented, dusty, well used.   It may have been as old as the men, though probably not.   It stood idle, unconcerned about the men and their activity.   It stood on its two iron legs leaning against its rubber-tired wheel, its legs bent almost double; perhaps it was kneeling, not standing.   Empty, its mouth gaped open toward the sky.   Its wooden handles, not quite parallel, trailed off irrelevantly behind it, like the wingbones of a plucked goose.   Its nose pointed off across the street, diagonally, wondering perhaps what lay around the corner.   We would find out before it, I thought.

The men were contemplating a large roughly triangular rock whose slightly domed top protruded a bit above the general level of the pavingstones.   It was about the size and shape of the barrow minus its legs, wheel, and handles. You might say it was the positive of the negative within the wheelbarrow.   They were made for one another.   You could tell the workmen knew that.   You felt the reason for their hesitancy was not fatigue, it was pleasure in the contemplation of this solid geometry.   Stone will fit barrow; it's only a question of putting them together.   Stone and wheelbarrow have no interest in the matter; they've done without one another for years.   There is pleasure in accomplishment, but pleasure is animate, distinguishes animate from inanimate.   Or so we animated think, we animatedly think.

The rope was new, unlike the wheelbarrow. It was yellow plastic of some kind, clearly new and quite unpleasant. The yellow plastic was soft to the touch, a little slimy even, but underneath that quality the rope was harsh, its unnatural strands hard and unforgiving. The rope was stupid, the men were attentive and capable, the rock was old and wise, the wheelbarrow was experienced and resigned to what would come.

Oh look, oh my, after so long time underground, nothing seen, not much heard, only the vibrations from above to keep you interested, here I am breaking surface. Those soft nimble things with their iron bars, I know iron when I feel it, neighbor iron. Why is this happening; why are those soft things doing this to me. I have been inseparable from my soil, the iron and copper things bent around me, for no reason was I ever moved before since the great settling first left me here; why is this happening now. One never knew one had never moved; without motion there is no awareness of its possibility. It's called burial for a reason though I can hardly be expected to know. Another sudden lurching, upended, brought completely into the daylight; then another respite. That empty thing, my iron shirt.

You could say rock and wheelbarrow were made for one another, though rocks of course are not made but (at least in this case) dug, and wheelbarrows like so many industrial products are made for generalized use, no designer can foresee every possible use to which his design is put, better then to leave all such consideration out of the picture. A triangle of footing: wheel and legs. Two handles for the two hands, long enough for optimal leverage and both ease and control when in use. The barrow itself: sloping, let the weight be carried near the wheel, facilitate dumping, enable steering.

It was the easiest thing he'd done all day. (Yesterday he'd done nothing: general strike.) The rock was exposed to the day, its top surface swept, a runneling ditch picked out around it.   Very unlikely there'd be further complications below. An iron gas-pipe and a couple of old rubberized or asphalted cables skirted it, the pipe even having crowded up against it in some long-ago major vibration, a bomb perhaps during the war, even a serious collision might have done it, say a bus and a dump-truck. But the rock was fully exposed and should come out without much trouble; the iron bars were up to the job. But they'd need rope. To tell the truth, they might not need rope, they could almost certainly get by without rope, and if it turned out they did need it they could make a run back to the yard though they'd have to explain, most likely, why they'd gone out without any. Better to step into this shop, buy some.

9. Tasting metal notes in coffee.

GRANADA: AFTERNOON, CLEAR, not too hot.   The American girl in the cafe.

Two tables away, two men at a table playing cards, one of them with a strange bagpipy thing hanging from the back of his chair. Remember the day my purse was stolen from the back of my chair: never do that again! Though that was in Seville, busy street, café table on busy street, toward evening, getting darker, lots of people walking around the tables... it's so quiet here, no one on the street, only the waiter in the doorway, those two men playing cards. I'll have tea. Wine? No, tea.

The waiter is very handsome for an older man. Nicely dressed too. It is so different here everyone always dressed rather nicely makes you want to take better care of yourself of everything in fact. Keep things in order as she has always told me to do. Tops in one place skirts, shorts in another. Pants. His pants well pressed from behind; apron hides everything in front. The long black apron, the pressed black pants, the worn shiny black shoes. One hand behind his back. Sometimes a smile, then it's gone.

He's brought the wooden box of tea, wooden box of tea for me. Envelopes; tea bags: English breakfast, mint, jasmine, Darjeeling, I bet they all taste the same. Floor-sweepings, he always called it, floor-sweepings tea. The afternoon in Paris when we tasted each others' teas: Darjeeling, Lapsang Souchon, Jasmine (mine), his black black black Lapsang too strong, tannic you know, fur on your teeth. *No, gracias, sin limón.* But I'll put the sugar cube in my purse, he always says, you never know when you may meet a horse.

Such a long drive it was and so boring at first and then so magical, driving through the water, windows open, sound of water, slow through the water, not knowing where we'll sleep, sea somewhere out on the left, toward the mysterious town with the fort. The oldest city in Europe, he said, settled by the Phoenicians before there was Rome. Imagine that, a time before there was Rome. So much I don't know. The day in Itálica, I knew about it a long time ago but never went, I should be more curious, I should travel more, I should learn things, but he says there's plenty of time, you work hard at what you do, there's always time to learn, there will always be things you don't know, the trick is to know what you want to know. And then learn it. Or find it. Roman theater or arena is it in Itálica where all the stones and pines are. And the café, lady on her horse. It's all studios, cafés, the crowded small apartment, work and study, now the back seat of the rented car, hotel rooms, cafés. Ah there she is under the plane-tree just standing there, tired maybe. Should I count, even though I'm sitting still. Still at the table. And she is still, still standing, standing under the plane-tree with its beautiful mottled bark. Mottled shade on the pavement underneath. She sees me, smiles, waves, comes toward me. Make space at the table. The men quietly play cards, the waiter stands in the doorway he sees she is coming but does not rush, the purse can hang on this chair, there is no danger here. Sometimes I know the count; often I don't. In Itálica the little boy ran toward the white plaster wall, jumped to see how high he could kick against the wall. Dirty marks on the wall, and everyone disapproved, you could see it, but no one interfered.

She smiled at her daughter, pulled the chair away from the table, set her handbag on the table, sat down at the table. How is your day so far? We were in the garden again. I walked back to meet you. He's at the fort, the round fort. Carlos Five, she reminds me, though I know it perfectly well, just didn't see any reason to say it. He's admiring the proportions. I think, she leans forward as if this is not to be mentioned too loud, that he even counts sometimes.

The marks getting thicker and heavier. Only mud I hope. Oh: the chair makes too much noise scraping. Forty-three times he kicked the wall. Yes: of course he counts: how else would he know. This to that, height to width, short side to long side. How many columns at the front of the temple; how many columns at the side. Quick: what's nine times seven? I never knew. But I know she won't want to have tea. A glass of wine probably, maybe sherry. Oh my god she's ordered coffee.

Nice to see her drinking tea, her mother thinks, looking down at the little cup of coffee the waiter has brought, adding the sugar cube, breaking it up with the tip of the spoon, the bowl pointed a little perhaps for that reason, or is it an egg-spoon, stirring methodically clockwise. This Spanish coffee never as good as Italian. No: to a different taste. When in Rome; when in Granada. Still, a metallic taste, maybe the spoon. How is it made, I wonder. Boiled, probably, in an aluminum pot, probably.

The shadows grew longer, too long to lie neatly in the street.

10. Dad drunk; pigeons.

HOED ANOTHER FOUR rows of vines before breakfast, and mowed some afterward. Set out peppers, lettuces, and onions. What fine days they were, and what fine weather; it's this weather reminds me of those days. I suppose every paisano here enjoys days like those. Think of this place as hot and dry, dry hot and windy, but they're born to it. Look at those gardeners with their ladder, ladder and cart haven't changed in centuries. Same contraption probably built these walls. Tempo is what makes the difference. That stone in Barcelona, men standing over it in the morning, same men standing in same place after lunch, nothing moved. Seemed impossibly inefficient at the time: but what's the hurry? Only the pigeons seemed to move fast, rising in a flurry, you wonder for what reason, bursting into the sky, flying off somewhere, flying back, circling, setlling back down again in the same place. What's the point? Does each pigeon return to his own place? But they all look alike. The stones, I've read, are numbered, and marked with stonecutter's marks. So they'll be put in the right place, according to plan? How was that done without blueprints? Primitive tools, steady intelligence.

We should plan a picnic lunch; then stopped at some nice place on the road. That ruined farmhouse for example where I climbed to where the roof had been for that photo of the mountain, a giant's head, made me think of Hill of Howth, riverrun, from swerve of shore, good Spanish ham and manchego, some olives, some bread. She doesn't like raw onions, so cool, so crisp. A bottle of wine of course.

Dad always had a bottle in the car, at least one.   Door
pocket, under the seat, glove compartment.   Dad drunk so
often, dead drunk, dad drunk.   Funny much of the time,
because when you're a teen-ager the tragedy doesn't strike
you.   Well, tragedy's not quite the word.   Pathetic really.
After that day I wrestled him down it didn't matter any
more.   Let him get drunk, long as I don't get killed in a
stupid accident.   Too bad we can't keep a bottle nice and
cold; too much trouble to pack ice and all that.   Mesón de
Jamón everywhere in Madrid but not likely here in Tarifa.
Anyway Cadiz tonight, Seville tomorrow, no need to picnic.
Pigeons! And gone again just as fast! Are there swifts here,
I wonder, why wonder that, I wonder if there are swifts
here, to gather in clouds and fly down the chimneys.   Each
of us wonders completely different things, and no way of
knowing about the others.   Where is that café I wonder?
Steep street, cypress trees all around, a little traffic picking
up again, won't take long to walk.   Ninety minutes I was in
that Carlos V fort, extraordinary place, and couldn't work
out height to diameter.   The question will always be there,
and there will always be a way to find the answer.   If it can
be done, she said, why do it.   There at the bottom of the
hill, past the shop selling those cheap guitars, do they see,
there they are sitting at the table, garçon leaning in the
doorway watching nobody, how long have they been
waiting there, look at those two guys playiing cards.

Touching Home: that would be a nice title.   Going Home a
cliché.   Touching Home: about the past, but baseball too,
drunk dad, cop friend, pigeons.   I'd forgotten his friend the
cop, I don't remember him, must have been very early.
Pigeons, yes: we had them in a pigeon-coop, chicken-wire
closing in a sort of balcony back porch, I suppose we lived
one or two storeys up. Seems to me you looked west toward
the bay off that porch. Roosevelt Street? McGee? A long
time ago, before the war, 1940 or '41.   A motorcycle; a

yellow Buick convertible. Snazzy. They dressed neatly in those days, hats, pleats, nothing synthetic, not yet. See them every night on my nightstand in that photo, her wool coat clutched at the throat, must have been cold, him jaunty in hightop pleated pants, fitted sweater-jacket, sailor's cap tilted at an angle. The street photographers in those days, why not here. I'd like a photo of those two women at that café table. Why not stop here under this plane-tree take out my camera. Look they see me smile now and wave what a great photo. Life is good.

11. Dry and thorny country.

TO GRANADA, MY RESPECTS.   We had planned a late start today, for though we are only at the beginning of our return south, we have short day's travel to tonight's stop.   Still it will not be an easy day & we were hoping for long sleep & leisurely breakfast, but were awakened in this peaceful inn by some idiot ringing a handbell, walking up & down the street, at dawn, before cock-crow — for Sunday mass, no doubt about it.   These people and their bells are noisier than the muezzins back in Arabia deserta, though thankfully less frequent. Well, nothing to be done, no going back to sleep, when it was light I found this quill to begin my report, begging your indulgence of its little substance, for our activity in Galicia is already well known (in spite of detractors), and our time on the road, as already stated, only just begun.

Even so we didn't leave the inn until nearly eleven — they were busy laying tables for a wedding feast, with flowers strewn prettily on the central table — & drove on through F_____ & G_____ to San Something, where our stock were watered & loads re-tied and tightened, for the day had grown quite warm, & promises to grow hotter in the coming days. We took nourishment there too, a real dinner in fact, so that we could save our provisions one more day, and took some rest, then took our way again on on small roads, past C_____ (the exact names will be supplied later, in any case these hamlets are called by different names by the various peasants we question on our way, some of them barely able to speak comprehensibly so badly raised they are & little traveled), then toward S

Something Else. We had traveled hardly a dozen miles by dark and at this rate are unlikely to reach al Andaluz within the year! I petition your authority to consider, not for our comfort but for the success of our cause and the considerations of the purse, let us take the chance of turning west for the sea and taking ship down coast and toward Cadiz whence the overland roads are well known and reasonably safe. The horseman leaves by first light I stop now.

A dozen leagues short of S Whatnot we found a beautiful country-house with rooms so we took one of course; one does not refuse the blessings of God. It was midmorning so we took some nourishment — cheese, the sour local wine, the rest of the bread we'd found so long ago at a farmstead — & rested an hour or so before going on to S.G. for our interviews and the banquet that customarily follows. The roast lamb was particularly good, as there are herbs growing here unknown elsewhere, not only are they strewn on the cooking flesh, but the beasts browse on them in the long days as they increase, so you might say the succulent meat is suffused with the land that has given rise to them. One day this land will prosper. Of the interview itself there is little more to report than you will already have heard. I am not taken seriously & make I fear a poor representative, my clothing has suffered from the hardships of overland travel in this dry and thorny country. (The sheep profit more than do I from the brambles and brush.) Fortunately it was an easy descent the short distance back to our room at the country house and here is good accommodation for the horse and pack mules and indulgent hospitality for us both.

But where do we go from here? My stories and the fool's music will not be well received in the city, where the residents think more about Vímara (who can't really present a serious threat, I think) than they do of their obligation to the glorious culture we continue to bring them. Though perhaps once we are properly appareled & can cut a better figure we will prevail; without a glass, day in and day out, we lose the habit of proper care at toilet. Were it not for the fool's constant company I would forget I am human, and I daresay I provide the same for him. He is gaunt and shabby, leading me to suppose I am the same; if we are not careful we will begin to look like their "saint" Jerome... The second horse has died. Now but men and mules, we must carry on.

12. In slower Italian.

HE DESERVES A BEER but where will we sleep. Everyone here, no matter how brokendown he looks, knows where he will sleep tonight. And who with? They all look like loners sitting with their glasses, work clothes, but do they work, or is this siesta time. Of course they may have been talking before we arrived. Groups of men standing at bars, talking, joking, falling silent when we arrive, when strangers arrive. Village behavior. Not hostile, not even suspicious, they simply live in a different world. A completely different world. And so they do not drink beer, they don't drink coffee, they smoke, they drink little glasses of something.

I would speak to this horse if I knew Spanish. *Guarda, ca-ballo, los alamos, así señorial...* Like so many Americans, the translator raises his voice, though only a little, when frustrated, speaking to someone who can't quite comprehend. But she, she speaks in slower Italian. Who would have guessed this lovely terrace was here behind the shabby café? The relationship of first sight to the interior and behind, bleak first awareness, engaging discovery, overwhelmingly satisfying conclusion.

When the Phoenicians first arrived was there vegetation. We owe it all, so they say, to the droppings of passing birds, unaware of their gift on their long flight, Nyasaland to Norway. What must those ancient shepherds have thought, eyes to the sky, the long lines and unfathomable clouds of birds overhead, apparently purposeful (like the sheep when on the move) yet utterly foreign, unknowable. Angels mediating earth and sky. How could they not fascinate us?

A hundred bollards at least stand like ninepins along the street leading to the esplanade, stunted urban poplars, no, pollarded willows like those along Dutch ditches, where Spaniards drowned like rats amazed these Protestants would flood their own land.   Seventy dollars for a hotel room and the slim breakfast.   Forty-nine airports I count, Melbourne to Moscow and home.   Seven cities of Cibola, cities of gold; seven legendary hills but not in Cadiz; nor here either.

She got it, I know, from me, the compulsion to count.   Steps in a flight; bollards in a row.   A compulsion to set things in order, is it, or a compulsion to know, to know a verifiable fact beyond discussion, way beyond argument.   He does so badly need to be in the right, me, I don't need to be right. (Well, be honest.   I do seem to need to be right.   He would say because of oldest child thing.)   Thing about facts is, one or the other must inevitably recognize the truth.   Blue; route; beverage: all individual matters.   Number of steps in flight: invariable.   One after another the dark little birds arrive from behind, angling gently down toward the shrubbery where they are attracted by what, by something to eat, their wingtips fluttering.   Amazing how they instinctively control the descent, avoid branches, find their proper position on the ground.   They too count, no doubt about it.   This an insight, sudden comprehension that all things in nature behave so, if behave is the right word. Intellection interferes with this, I think, especially male intellection, as it is instituted in social norms.   And yet architecture how could it be without this.   Imagine a flight of architects intuitively gathering, fingertips fluttering, each finding proper place in the lineup.   That day in San Francisco when the lawyer said Come just a little before four o'clock there's something I want to show you, and when I arrived he took me to the window and pointed, dozens of young men all in the same suits carrying the same briefcases walking in the same direction. We went to the bar: they were all drinking the same beer, Corona. I ordered Pinot grigio; he had a gin and tonic. What I admire in birds is not admirable in lawyers. Is anything admirable in lawyers. Respect for the truth when it can be established, and respect for the client and her view of the truth, that would be admirable.

The American girl stepped up to the table, come from hard to know where. Found a hotel? Great! What a pleasure, a daughter fluent in the language, street-smart, adaptable, comfortable with herself as I never was, that's not true, yes I was. But she doesn't have a man to deal with. Not that we know. Completely absorbed in her study, her work. I'd hoped for a good talk, try to understand her commitment to this, plans for the future, where will it lead.

13. Stones, birds, gods.

THIS WILL BE the hardest thing to do.   Casting off is the easiest.   Everything planned and arranged as best one can, goodbye to the woman and the kids, out from the harbor, wind behind us.   From then on nothing to do but coast along the coast, that's funny, that's why we say coast I suppose, coast down along the coast downwind, looking for whatever we find.   Why look for something we won't find? What kind of fool does that?   The only thing, the princess in her slippers at the stern, getting in the way, but no longer demanding things.   Doesn't take long to learn: be content with what's at hand.   And yet, look for whatever you'll find. At least she's good with the stories, and certainly knows her alphabet.   Nineteen, I think, and no longer pretty, but she'll be a problem just the same when we land at Tarifa.   Let's hope the winds are kind and the seas calm, she's never before been on open water.   Luff!   Haul!   They're still ashore, the seas will snap them out of it.

Those black rocks off shore: birds settling on them: more rocks beyond, submerged.   Where he foundered four years ago, no, five, taking all our stuff with him.   An old tuna pen perhaps.   They should set a cairn on it but no one can get anything like that together.   They get it done in Egypt and they say they manage such things in Crete; why not here? Different kind of people, all greek to me.   Barbarians. Good sailors though, if the princess tells true stories.   All I know is, you can't really know anything but what's in front of your eyes, and at sea, under the sun, you can't always depend even on that.   What was her story about?   Tying himself to the mast?   Who can believe such stories?   All that drivel about songs and sirens: the wind whistling through the lines, or those singing blowholes when the wind and water's right. Any sailor worth his salt knows about that but you can't expect a girl to, not even a princess. If she even is; but don't doubt your backers.

A sudden still; not the least bit of a breeze, the sail hangs useless. Becalmed. Be calm: we have oars but don't rush them out. Food and water have we plenty and the coast, the fertile coast, an easy swim away. Look how close the white sand below us. A school of fish below, a flock of birds above, and we suspended in between, not fish nor feathers. Time for a story? They turn toward the girl who lies back on her carpet, the points of her slippers indicating a cloudless sky. She yawns and they know that that indicates the story will be a true one. No one can know where the stories come from: they come effortlessly from within, I suppose — but her eyes roll up and to the left from time to time, perhaps a goddess we cannot see stands behind her, whispering the truth. What do we know of women's things. She's been guarded all this time, never out among the world of men, of trade, of travel. Only the women can have told her this.

The sea has not always been here. We came from the south, a land of trees and plains, we moved among the grasses and the trees, following game and the fruits in their seasons. Gods and men instructed us and we followed the advice of the old men and we learned about foods and medicines from the old women. Children came and went, died and were born, and we watched old people go away, and sometimes we followed. We always wandered north, suns rising on our right and setting on our left. We learned to tend the grasses behind the river's mud. Things became complicated, some of us had to concentrate. As an old woman knows the plants and the family names but nothing more, so others knew the stones and the needs of the gods, how to please the gods and follow the stars and the birds, but nothing practical. They have to be fed and well fed too, to say nothing of adornment, the rest of us wearing only a skirt, and that only after the blood begins. There were more and more of us until we could not be counted, and many went away, toward the sun as it rose in the morning. They went toward the sun and then the earth moved and the sea rushed in where the land had been low and flat, where the grasses had grown so faithfully. Even the priests were surprised; they had never dreamed of such a thing. The birds flew through the skies as they always had, the mountains where the sun goes down never changed, the river changed its course but the mud appeared as it always had but in different places. New kinds of fish appeared, big ones, good to eat when you could kill them but we had to learn how. It was a time to learn many new things, new ways to make boats, to tie ropes, to keep track of inventories. New gods came to replace the old ones who had died or been carried toward the morning sun. And — as many knots in a rope, that many boats carrying dates, behind ours. All these things.

14. Dusty bars and cafés.

IN CADAQUES AT A TABLE we drank a beer and watched the silent town. Suddenly a woman burst out from a building the other side of the street. She was thirty or forty, red blouse, tight dark skirt, high heels, and she ran amazingly fast up the steep street, away from us. Then a man burst out through the same door brandishing a kitchen knife. He ran after her, soon giving up.

In Avila the most amazing thing was the sound of the storks. Not the dark stone of the cathedral, the formidable city gate, not even Teresa's letter to John, I suppose, or maybe Ignatius, in a fine hand perfectly legible; nothing as amazing as the sound of the storks, beating their bills together with the sound of bamboo sticks. They nest on the rooftops beating their bills together, and snow lies all around.

In Toledo he thinks of El Greco. Did he suffer from astigmatism, he wonders; does that explain his distorted portraits, foretelling a Giacometti Modigliani? Only think of that marvelous little sculpture, Adam and Eve, nudes who lived centuries ago. She, however, while aware of El Greco, broods on the terrible landscape, the terrible drop to the river far below, where so many were killed in the Civil War, how ironic to call it civil.

In Zamora we were beset by mischievous boys who taunted us, dropped their pants at us, even threw rocks at us, when all we did to offend was walk about town taking photographs and being American, more American than we wanted to be, more American than we knew. There are two towns in Zamora, the new one of shops, hotels, and restaurants, and the old one of castle and church and museum. And the boys.

In Ronda the bullring and the bridge, the bridge high above a dizzying gorge, had the war come there as well? How could it not? A white city above the plain covered with olive trees, in the distance a mountain like a recumbent giant's head, a fallen giant, his body long since merged into the plain, making it fertile perhaps. And the woman at her work, caged birds all around her, smiling sweetly as we watched.

In Beisbol the dusty ceramics in their dusty warehouse-shops, and the deserted dusty main street with its dusty bars and cafés. The dust of centuries and clay. When did women first think of using clay? Women or men, men or boys? The American girl fingers a soap-dish idly, her fingertip counting the perforations.Two rows of four; or, four sets of two, of pairs. They are a pair, no, a couple, and I make three.

In Jerez the mouse waits. Nervous. Small and nervous, aware of the trick, wanting the wine, afraid of the man, what a life, but we all have to make a living. Outside a terrible rainstorm; inside only a patient tourguide, and American couple, and American girl. The reassuring scent of aging sherries, and afterward, lingering in a salon with good cheese, olives, bread, a small bottle of sherry, here in Jerez de la Frontera. Buy a souvenir!

In Salamanca as in Madrid the astonishing plaza, Mayor or Real, old men in the sun, old women in the shadows, young people walking hand in hand or standing in clusters scattered about, smoking or not smoking, rarely smiling though suddenly laughing, and around the corner the hidden smaller plaza aslant, and beyond that the university and the double cathedral. Now then as I was saying, the philosopher said as he returned to class from prison.

In Tarifa seventy-five words made of letters, letters from the twenty-six of the alphabet, brought here by mariners. Letters, fish, nets made of rope, clay pots to keep them in, and the dainty slippers reaching for the sand. All of it is all made of stories, stories heard from over the left shoulder, and overhead the steady birds herded this way or that according to where the stars are, above even the birds.

And, beyond, the spit dividing sea from ocean, waves and currents, tides and breezes, reaching back to Africa. Young men play in the wind.

15. A certain perfume.

YOU SMELL LIKE SPAIN, he said, as we got into his car at the airport. Yeah, I said, sweat and stale cigarette smoke. No, he said, it's more than that, I've often noticed it before, when people arrive from Spain, or when I land there — there's a characteristic smell. It's partly sweat and cigarette smoke, but there's a certain perfume, something that means Spain.

Maybe. I'd been wearing the same wool sportcoat, a Harris tweed, for a month. In normal weather it would have had a few days off, and maybe even a dry cleaning, but the weather was never normal. It had been cold. It was freezing when we left Madrid. I stowed my topcoat — wool, of course — in its travel bag just before getting on the airplane. Otherwise it was wool sweater, wool sport coat, all the way home..

Wool, sweat, ham, cigarette smoke, and no doubt the scent of sherry — I suppose there are those who would take offense at the combination, but to me it had grown familiar and even somewhat pleasant, the smell of being alive and even enjoying myself. Paintings and music are fine, but for intimate pleasures there's nothing like scents, fragrance, aroma. Alice B. Toklas named her second book *Aromas and Flavors*, and as a title it's hard to beat.

Still, when I stepped out of his car to open the gate, stepped out into a night that while cool seemed positively balmy after Spain, a deep night, no moon, plenty of stars overhead, and the scent of new green grass on the hillsides, the cattle sheds a mile to the south, the peach and plum and nectarine trees in bloom — I was home. I could smell so many of the details: the shale on the road, the decomposed-granite patio, the damp teak patio table, the rosemary blossoms, the laurel tree when I brushed against it.

O

They had come from the south, a land of trees and plains, they had moved among the grasses and the trees, following game and the fruits in their seasons. and, always, the birds. Gods and men instructed them and they followed the advice of the old men and they learned about foods and medicines from the old women. Others had turned toward the morning sun but we kept it on the right until the water stopped us and there we stayed until the big water came and most of us were lost.

Then slowly we built as the strongest men wanted, and then there were gods and priest, scribes and lawyers, beeswax tablets. The busy docks and the boatloads of dates, disappearing, and others arriving, who knows from where, stone, wine, wool. The men always leaving us, only the boys and old men and priests and lawyers staying and always demanding.

.

Her slipper hit the sand before I could warn her, footsteps everywhere but soon washed away. Beyond there were other girls, playing with a ball, all good-looking, one more beautiful than the others. They ignored us. She went off into a grove of trees, to pray, she said, and we heard singing. Then she came back to the boat wading out to it with no trouble and climbing in without help. She took her place in the stern and remained silent as we pushed back out from the shore. The skies were clear the sea calm and there were no birds. It would be two more days before the crossing to the northern shore. None of this was the least bit difficult; we will arrive without having lost any of the cargo.

• •

Our Roman legacy everywhere.   Discipline, poetry, and arenas. Priests, lawyers, and strong men to push things into order, as a countryman with his dog herds his sheep. It isn't difficult: ants, bees, geese, deer, the stupid sheep fall into place quite naturally.   They swerve together, round and square, old and young, following the strong men. Set things in their ordained places: slaves heed supervisors, who listen to the augur, who consults birds, flying between gods and men.

Less slowly, they built as the strongest men wanted, and the gods, now more numerous but weaker, looked on, or they did not.   The boats brought new gods, some more appealing than others of course, like every other cargo. But we had our needs: sweet things, and wine, and bread; games, and dancing, and entertainers; and places to gather, places for all these things, temples and arenas, theaters and gymnasia, for like sheep, geese, and bees we are social animals and swerve together.

.
. .

Now but men and mules, we carried on, arriving finally at the coast where after three days the winds were propitious & we cast off, beating south along the coast, then east with the tide toward Cadiz.   What pleasure once again to be clean & properly shorn & shaven, to wear decent cloaks though not new of course, to look forward to our arrival among the Lions, & to hear the Griffin sing again…

Ninety-seven days & nights have we been on our journey; we have lost many horse; we have eaten strange even unthinkable things; we have known curious men with strange ideas & opinions about which we thought it best to remain silent, not to provoke discussion leading likely to quarrel for we were in no position to defend ourselves & were, in fact, at the mercy of those we met on our travels. As you know it is better to agree & move on than to dispute; there are places on God's world for men of every belief, & many swerves of the roads lead to the one final end.

O

The American girl smiled…

Translator's notes

LITTLE IS KNOWN OF the French author Jean Coqt, whose curious book *Skagen: un roman de l'Europe* was found in typescript in a used-book shop in Grenoble. The bookseller was glad to part with it. Internet searches have turned up nothing.

I have tried to translate the typescript faithfully, but the original French is idiosyncratic, and some curious lapses in style have resulted. I have mostly left Spanish and Galician words (and some in other languages) untranslated.

Page 1: *Carryl:* Charles Carryl, author of the children's book *Davy and the Goblin* (1884).

Page 15: *Vallée des Merveilles:* the valley in the Alps north of Menton, famous for its petroglyphs. *Het Loo:* the summer palace and park in Apeldoorn, Netherlands.

Page 18: *acequias:* tile-lined irrigation channels running among trees in a grove. *Gaita:* a kind of bagpipe.

Page 19: *De rerum natura:* the great philosophical poem of Lucretius. (This sentence breaks off without a stop in the original.)

Page 20: *Tintin and the Secret of Literature:* the book by Tom McCarthy (2006).

Page 28: *Itálica:* founded by the Romans in 206 BCE, the birthplace of the emperor Trajan.

Page 35, *Vímara:* Vímara Peres (c. 820-873), Count of Portugal. A greater threat than the narrator knew, he managed to expel the Moors from Galicia in the year 868.

set in Baskerville and Deco Type Naskh

ear : press : 2014